from

LOVE

to

ASHES

Was it chance that
brought them together?

IVY LOVE

from

LOVE

to

ASHES

Was it chance that
brought them together?

From Love To Ashes
Copyright © 2019 by Ivy Love.

Cover design and Formatting by Jersey Girl Design, *www.jerseygirl-design.com*

First Edition: May 2019

This is a work of fiction. Names, characters, places, and incidents are either the product of the author's imagination or are used fictitiously, and any resemblance to actual persons, living or dead, business establishments, events or locales is entirely coincidental.

All rights reserved. This e-book is licensed for your personal enjoyment only. This e-book may not be re-sold or given away to other people. If you would like to share this book with another person, please purchase an additional copy for each recipient. If you are reading this book and did not purchase it, or it was not purchased for your use only, then please return to retailer and purchase.

DEDICATION

To all those that believe in love and happy endings.

ACKNOWLEDGMENTS

I tend to forget to acknowledge people in these things and for that I am sorry in advance. It's not on purpose, it's just that I suck sometimes. Please know that if I forgot you, it was not intentional.

MJ Fields, you are always the first person I thank. Thank you for giving me the push I needed to do this. You are a wonderful friend; bad ass author and I am so happy to have you in my life.

Thank you to Bobbie, Jamie, Laurie, and Paige for our crazy conversations. I love that no matter how far apart we are, our friendship survives.

Thank you to Juliana Cabrera of Jersey Girls for creating a beautiful cover for this book. I have had such a great time working with you. I've been in love with this cover for so long, I'm glad, I got to use it!

Thank you to my late-night sprinting buddy Ashley Erin. I love our sessions and they are so motivating!

Thank you to TC Matson for the advice and encouragement. I truly appreciate your friendship and our conversations.

Thank you to my betas, for reading, editing and giving me feedback. I appreciate all your comments and love.

Thank you to my Imps! I am so grateful for all of you and happy that I have you to throw around ideas and just chat about random fun stuff. Thank you for being here with me on this journey. Thank you for all you do.

Thank you to all the blogs who take the time to reply to my messages, who like, share, review, tweet, etc., about my books. I cannot begin to express my appreciation for you. Please know I am very grateful.

Thank you to my husband who blindly supports this passion I have. For sharing my books, when I'm too shy to and buying me supplies when I need them. I appreciate it more than you know.

Last-but-not-least, thank you to you. Yes, you, the reader for picking up this book. I hope you enjoy it as I much I did.

Love, Ivy

PLAYLIST

These are a few of the songs that I kept on repeat while writing Cassie and Colt's story. I hope you enjoy them as much as I do.

La La La by Naughty Boy & Sam Smith
Sucker by Jonas Brothers
Happier by Marshmello & Bastille
Naked by James Arthur
Too Good at Goodbyes by Sam Smith
Tequila by Dan + Shay
Collide by Howie Day
Stone Cold by Demi Lovato
Let Her Go by Passenger
Mercy by Shawn Mendes
Don't Go Breaking My Heart by Backstreet Boys

CHAPTER ONE

Cassie

"I stare at the ring on the dresser a sense of dread growing in my stomach. That ring represents so many things. Things, I wish I could redo, take back, and forget. I know I need to put it on, but I hate it. It brings back feelings of despair and an overwhelming fear of being trapped, among other things I wish I had never experienced. I swallow and compose myself before reaching down and sliding it slowly onto my finger. Each inch it slides up is a stark reminder of the shame, humiliation and pain I bear.

I look in the mirror one last time and finish getting ready to go out. I try to tell myself I deserve a night out. A night with no guilt or fear. I run my fingers lightly across my neck, tilting my head slightly. Inspecting myself for scars and bruises that I know, no longer exist. I want to be able to go out and enjoy myself. If it means putting the ring on, I'll do it, just for one night. One night of freedom.

I breathe deeply, compose my face, check my makeup and outfit before grabbing my purse and walking to the door. I make sure my alarm system is armed as I leave for the night. I'm going to a bar right down the road that way if I want to get drunk, I can safely walk home.

I'm hoping tonight will push the deafening roar of darkness back for just a minute. I walk briskly down the road ignoring everyone around me but remaining conscious of potential danger. It's something I've become accustomed to doing over the past years. I push open the bar door to a burst of warm air, tobacco and loud music. The bar is dim and the pressure filling my chest loosens slightly, allowing me to breathe a bit easier.

I walk up to the bar and before I have the chance to sit down, I hear her yelling.

"Oh my god! Cassie, is that you? No, I must have died and gone to heaven," a female voice, squeals.

I laugh, a sound I haven't heard in quite some time and watch as my once best friend, Taylor, comes barreling around the bar. She wraps me in her arms and squeezes me tightly.

"Holy fuck, I've missed you, Cassie. Where have you been? Are you okay? I have a million questions for you," she fires off, releasing me from her death grip.

I watch her as her eyes glance at my hand and her brows furrow.

"Next question, why the hell are you wearing that?"

"Good lord woman can one of your questions be what do you want to drink?" I smile.

"Jack and coke, still your thing?" she asks, walking back behind the bar.

"Please, and to answer your rapid-fire questions. I've been hiding. No, I'm not okay, but I'm getting there. This is for protection," I say, wiggling my hand, "and without a doubt I've missed you."

She places my drink in front of me. "Damn right you missed me. I still need to work but don't go, enjoy the music and I'll get you drunk. Also, if you even think about leaving, don't, but if you do at least say goodbye."

"Promise," I smile.

I watch as she walks away and shake my head. Ever since the day I met her, I knew she was going to be a spitfire. She is unapologetically bold and brash and doesn't care who likes her. It makes her a great bartender, but an even better friend. She's fiercely loyal once she takes you under her wing.

I love that girl and I really did miss her. Hopefully, tonight is a night of new beginnings and I'll be able to start coming out more. But I don't want to get ahead of myself.

For now, I'll just enjoy my drink and the steady beat of the music. I sit there swaying in my own world for a few minutes before the first interruption happens.

"Well, hello there," a smooth voice says. "How are you this fine evening?"

I look up to see a dark-haired, thirty something year old smirking down at me. I know exactly what he's looking for and I have no intention of giving it to him. I glance over at Taylor and see her smirking. I look down and clear my throat to keep myself from laughing.

"Hi, there. I'm doing alright," I smile, slowly lifting my drink, flashing my ring.

I watch his eyes deflate as he spots the ring. "Um, yeah, I'm cool. You know what I just saw my friend come in. Have a good night," he mumbles, walking off.

"You too," I call out, with a grin.

I quickly down the rest of my drink. If this is any indication of how the night is going to go, I'm going to need another drink. But I'm going to start getting doubles. I look down the bar and wait to catch Taylor's eye. She's beautiful and tall, with blonde hair that flows down her back and sky-blue eyes to match. On top of that, her curves fall in all the right places, at least according to her sexual partners. Her most prized possession a bad ass, rose bush tattoo on her right upper thigh.

I watch as she works, smiling and flirting with everyone she talks with. I envy her. She is unafraid and I wish I could absorb that trait from her. She has no problem finding suitors, but she says she's waiting for the right one. I can't wait to meet the person that finally takes her down.

The bar is packed tonight and when I finally get her attention I hold up two fingers for a double. She nods her head and I wait for her to make her way back to me.

"Hey there, this seat taken?" a twenty-something, blonde asks before sitting.

"Nope, just know I'm not available," I smile.

"Well, that's alright we can just have a conversation, right?" he asks.

"Of course. I just don't want to give you the wrong impression, especially when there are several women at the other end of the bar glaring at me."

"Here you go, hon. You good?"

I nod, "Yes, still good. Thanks for checking on me."

I put my hand on the guys arm, "stop looking at them."

"Ooo, are you going to play wing woman for him?" Taylor asks, excitedly.

"Yes, if he'll be cool," I smirk.

"Hey, I'm cool," he retorts.

"Good, then just chill a second and we'll help you with the ladies, as long as you promise you're not an asshole," I say, sternly.

"Scouts honor, I'm no asshole," he says, in complete seriousness.

"Were you even a scout?" Taylor asks.

"For a month," he says, with a straight face.

We all laugh and out of the corner of my eye I see the girls looking our way.

"Which girls are they?" Taylor asks, looking around.

"The blonde and brunette at the end towards the right. They're looking this way."

"You, Mr. Calm and Cool just hang here for another minute and then walk away. My guess is they'll be following you within a few seconds," I grin.

He laughs and I look at him. If I was in the market for someone, I might be interested in him.

"What?" he asks.

"Nothing," I say, "But you should be good to go. It was nice to meet you."

"You too. Thanks for the help. If it doesn't work out, I'll be back," he says, standing up.

"Don't worry, it'll work. Enjoy your night. Remember don't be an asshole," I grin.

"Scouts honor," he smiles, walking away.

Taylor and I discreetly watch as the two girls hustle through the crowd to introduce themselves to the guy who just left my side. She and I laugh.

"Why'd you help him Cassie?"

"He didn't give off a pervy vibe and he seemed nice enough, so I figured what harm could it do?"

I watch her roll her eyes, "Lord woman, just drink and behave."

"Yes, ma'am!"

I lift my drink and sip.

CHAPTER TWO

Colt

I noticed her the moment she walked into the bar. I think anything with a dick within ten miles immediately perked up when she walked in the room.

Her hair is dark, chocolate brown that sparkles when the light hits it. She's wearing heels and doesn't look very tall but has hips and an ass that are begging to be grabbed. Her shirt is low enough to tease the fact that she's well-endowed up top as well. She's a man's fantasy come to life, but instead of walking in like she owns the place, she sneaks in quietly as if she's trying to avoid attention.

Unfortunately, for her, she radiates and when she smiles it's hard not to stare. Even though she has a rock on her hand suitors are still trying their odds.

I watch in fascination as she politely declines advance after advance. Nobody leaves her side upset though. Embarrassed, maybe, but not upset. She's soft-spoken even though the atmosphere doesn't call for it. She seems to be the opposite of her bartender friend.

The whole time I'm watching her I notice she twists her ring, almost as if she's uncomfortable wearing it. She hasn't checked her phone once, either. You'd think if you're married you would at least send a text or something, but her phone hasn't come out once.

The bartender brings over another drink and I feel like this is my chance. I get up from my seat and make my way over to where she's sitting.

"Hi, I'm Colt. I've been sitting across the bar watching you turn down guys, so I figured I'd come over and just keep you company. I don't need a wing woman; I'm just looking for some conversation. Think you can handle that?"

I watch her throw her head back and laugh.

"Okay, you can sit here. By the way, thanks for the stalker honesty," she says.

"Well, you know, I wanted to give you an out in case you were watching me," I tease.

I watch her bartender friend come over, "Hey you were on the other side."

"I was, but the company is so much better over here. Is that okay?"

She pauses, "Yes, I think it is. You want another?"

"Please," I say.

I watch them share a look. "Have I been approved?"

"We'll see," the bartender says, putting my drink down in front of me. "I'm Taylor, by the way, the pretty thing you're sitting next to is Cassie. Be nice to her."

"Thank you, I'll be a perfect gentleman," I say.

"I'm sure you will," Taylor says.

"Cheers," I say, raising my glass to Cassie.

She raises her glass, "What are we toasting to?"

"To new friends and adventures."

"Adventures, huh?" she says, with a raised eyebrow.

"Alright, I'll toast to that."

I grin, tapping her glass lightly as I sip my whiskey.

"So, how do I rank so far on the company scale, better or worse than those that have come before?"

She laughs, "You know what it's too early to tell right now but so far so good."

"Good. I saw you play wing woman and turn away lots of men, are you still having fun?"

"Damn, you really were stalking me," a slight hesitation entering her voice.

"Sorry, not stalking, but the moment you walked in the door it was hard to take my eyes off you. You demanded attention, even though you clearly didn't want any."

I watch her eyes soften slightly, "That's kind of sweet. You could tell I was trying to be invisible?"

"I don't know if I'd say invisible," I say, slowly. "But definitely like you were just trying to mind your own business and not be bothered."

"Hmm, interesting," she murmurs, before sipping her drink.

I watch as the lip of the cup brushes against her lips. I know I told her I was just keeping her company, but I'm suddenly very jealous of a cup.

"To answer your earlier question, yes, I'm still having fun. Nobody that came by was particularly aggressive, so I didn't need to sic Taylor on them," she says with a chuckle.

"Yeah, your girl is a beast it seems," I nod.

"She is. She'd do anything for her friends, and she has very few people she calls friends. She is loyal to a fault, even when it may not be in her best interest," she shrugs, shaking her head.

I reach over and touch her arm, "Hey, it's very rare in life when you have someone, anyone that will be there for you like that. You should be happy to have that in your life."

She glances down at my hand and then up at my face, her brown eyes sparkling as they gaze into mine. It hits me immediately; I feel like I've been punched right in the gut.

CHAPTER THREE

Cassie

The second he puts his hand on me, the world goes silent and a shot of electricity shoots through my body. I can't hear a word he's saying; I know his lips are moving, but I can only feel this connection he's created between the two of us.

It's fascinating and terrifying all at the same time. I want to move my arm, but I'm frozen. I push through the fog that's clouding my brain to try and formulate an appropriate response. I try to look him in the eyes, but it doesn't help. His grey eyes penetrate mine, staring intently. I wish I knew what he was thinking, instead I find my voice.

"We should be so lucky," I manage to choke out.

Thankfully, he removes his hand and the electricity that was penetrating me to my very core has vanished. I gasp aloud at the physical loss but try to quickly cover it by shakily grabbing my drink.

"Why whiskey?" he asks.

"I'm not sure. I don't think I've ever had someone push it on me, but I've always loved the taste of whiskey more than anything else. What about you?"

"Whiskey is the family drink. You can't go to one of

our functions without seeing or being offered whiskey. So, the taste kind of grew on me. Now I just order it out of habit," he says, reflectively.

We sit quietly for a few minutes, listening to the music and watching the people mill around. I see him go to speak and drop my hand on his arm. The moment I touch him, the connection we had before is back. It shakes me for a moment, but I regain my composure quickly.

"No personal questions, okay? Just random ones if you're going to ask them. Please."

As soon as I'm done talking, I lift my hand and break the connection.

"Okay, deal," he says, studying my face. "But you have to answer any question as long as it doesn't fall into the 'too personal' category."

I look at him, lifting an eyebrow, "Deal."

"Ice cream cone or cup?" he asks.

I burst out laughing and find him looking at me, trying to hold back a smile.

"It depends on my mood. If I want sprinkles or anything like that, then a cup otherwise a cone."

"Pro sprinkle or con sprinkle?" I ask.

"Is there a right answer?"

"What do you think?" I say, solemnly.

"Pro sprinkle, definitely pro," he says, quickly.

"Good answer," I grin. I give myself an internal shake. What am I doing? Am I flirting with this man and if so, why am I doing it?

"Cereal or eggs for breakfast?"

"Neither, I don't usually eat breakfast. You?"

"Both," he says firmly.

"Figures, you're a breakfast person, you're probably a morning person too," I pause. "Running or swimming?"

"Both," he says, again, shrugging nonchalantly.

"Yeah, I'm not surprised, you're fine as hell," I mumble to myself.

"What'd you say?" he asks, over the music.

"Oh, um, you can't tell," I stutter.

"Thank you. I work out, sometimes," he grins.

I lift my drink and sip, forcing myself to stay quiet.

We continue playing the game for several hours. People come and go, but Taylor keeps filling our drinks and I realize I'm actually enjoying myself. Something I haven't done in a long time. It's a weird feeling, being happy. I've forgotten what it feels like to be carefree and happy.

"Last call," Taylor calls out.

"Oh wow. I can't believe we talked all night." I look around at the emptying bar.

"Am I that bad of company?" he teases.

I blush, "No, it's just, I wasn't expecting to stay out this late."

"What? You weren't going to walk me out to my car?" Taylor admonishes, teasingly.

"You're a grown ass woman, you got this," I say, sticking out my tongue. "Besides I was trying to leave you with the bill," I laugh.

She slaps the bill in front of me, "Maybe if you'd offered to walk me to my car this would have disappeared," she grins, sauntering away.

I flip her off as I reach for the bill, but before I can grab it Colt's fingers snake out and grab it right from under me.

"My treat," he shrugs, pulling out his card to pay.

"Oh, you don't have to do that."

"Please, it's my pleasure. I had a wonderful time I would be happy to pay tonight."

"Are you sure? I don't want you to think I'm taking advantage of you. I'm more than comfortable paying for my own drinks."

He smiles, "You're cute, but no I'm a big boy and I'm choosing this."

"Well, thank you and thank you for keeping me company tonight."

I stand and grab my things.

"I don't come out often, but when I do, this is usually one of my favorite spots."

"Well, maybe I'll see you around?" he asks, hopefully.

"Maybe." I know he's hinting toward getting my number, but I don't want to give it up that easily. Besides, if I know Taylor, and I do, she'll end up giving it to him. Especially once she realizes he's paying.

"Have a good night, get home safe," I wave.

He shakes his head grinning. "You too."

"Bye, Taylor!" I yell.

"Bye, bitch. Expect a call," she calls back.

"I'd expect nothing less," I yell back walking toward the door.

I'm tipsy, but I know I need to focus on my surroundings. The walk home is cold, short and quiet. I make it to my place and do my usual check of my condo. After making sure nothing has been moved, I breathe a sigh of relief.

I lock the door and immediately turn on my alarm again. As soon as I hear my home is armed, I look down at the gaudy ring on my hand and peel it from my finger, placing it back on the dresser. My heart immediately feels lighter.

CHAPTER FOUR

Colt

I watch as she walks out of the bar. She is beyond beautiful and truly has no idea.

"Alright, Romeo, are you paying?" Taylor asks.

"Yes, ma'am," I say, handing over my card.

She makes a little noise and goes to swipe my card for our drinks. She drops the receipt and a pen in front of me.

"What's your deal?" she asks.

"What do you mean?"

"I don't think you're an idiot, Colt, so don't play dumb."

"No, I'm not, but I think you and I both know your friend is beautiful."

"She is. We both saw the way everyone looked at her when she walked in."

"Agreed. She's hard not to miss. In answer to your question, I'm talking to a gorgeous girl, who left without giving me her number and I'm hoping to be able to talk to her again."

"Why her? You're not a bad looking guy. You could have had any girl here."

"I saw her trying to enjoy a drink by herself and decided to try and help her. It just happened we kicked it off and talked all night."

She stares at me suspicion in her eyes.

"I won't apologize for a good night of conversation."

"You want her number, don't you?" she asks.

"You know I do," I say, my eyes unwavering from hers.

"What are you going to tip me?" she asks, bluntly.

"I'm not buying her phone number, but I think your service was excellent, so here you go." I reply, filling out the receipt.

I watch as she picks up the receipt and looks.

"Damn, at least you're not cheap."

She sighs, looking me up and down, "You're definitely easy on the eyes. I can see why she was smiling so much. But that doesn't mean I trust you."

I go to speak, but she holds up her hand.

"That being said, I haven't seen her out in such a long time, nor have I seen her smile that much in, in I can't remember how long. So, I'll give you her number, but understand if you hurt her on purpose, I'll find you and hurt you."

"Understood," I say, lifting my hands in defense.

She slides a piece of paper over to me with Cassie's number on it.

"Now get out of my bar so I can close up."

"Thank you. I'll be back."

"I expect you will be. Drive safe and I'll see you soon," she says, waving me out.

I contain my smile as I walk out of the bar.

As soon as I'm out the door, my phone begins to ring.

"Yes?" I ask, without looking at the caller id.

"You know Taylor is going to eat you alive if she ever finds out, right?"

"Yes, Red, I know," I sigh.

His name isn't Red, it's a nickname he's earned from his red hair. His actual name is Timothy, but nobody calls him that. Red fits him better, he doesn't really look like a Timothy or a Tim.

"Are you sure you still want to do this?" he asks.

"I don't know is Chris going to try and hit on her again and then fuck it up?"

I hear yelling in the background. "I think that's a no. He says he went with what your lady said so he didn't blow his cover and it worked."

"Yeah, whatever," I say.

"I'm not playing mediator," Red says.

I can tell he is talking to both Chris and I and I'm not in the mood to get into an argument.

"Look, I'm not thrilled about this, but this is what needs to happen. She has no clue what she's gotten herself into."

"Yeah, well, the plan wasn't to talk to her all night, now was it?" Red asks.

"Look, I wasn't planning on talking to her all night, but it worked out didn't it?"

I can hear him sighing in the background.

"I'm going to say this again, are you sure you want to do this? I'm sure we can figure out another way to get what we need, without you having to do this. Taylor is going to kick your ass into next week, when she finds out what you've done." He pauses, "Though, I want to be around when that happens, because that is a show I want to see. On top of that she seems like my type of woman, the kind of woman who can fend for herself. You know if things work out and we all get out of this unscathed, I want a proper introduction."

I laugh, "Yeah, I'll get right on that introduction. Regarding everything else, yes, I'm sure. It's what needs to be done. I'm in it now. We all are."

CHAPTER FIVE

Cassie

I SIT ON THE COUCH DRYING MY HAIR AS THE TELEVISION plays reruns of one of my favorite shows. I'm not really paying attention to what's on though. Instead, I'm reliving this evening. I am still in awe over the fact I went out tonight and had fun. The last time I went out and had fun was before I met Jay.

I shudder as I remember my last encounter with him. His last words to me as he was walking out the door were, *"You'll regret this. Nobody says no to me."*

It was the last time we spoke. For a few weeks, I was afraid to leave my house. Jay isn't someone who says something without a meaning, but nothing's ever happened. When I finally got the courage to leave the house, I had the feeling someone was watching me. I could never prove it, but it was an uncomfortable feeling that followed me everywhere I went. I didn't leave the house for over a year after that.

Tonight, was an anomaly, but I wanted to leave the house to celebrate my birthday. I haven't been out to celebrate anything in so long, I decided to take a chance. It turns out it was worth it.

My phone vibrates against the table jerking me from my daydream. I open it to see a text message from Colt.

Cassie, hope you don't mind. Taylor gave me your number. – C

I shake my head and type out a quick message to Taylor.

Really? You couldn't hold out at least day, T? – Cass

My phone buzzes back within seconds.

Nope, he was a good tipper – T

I laugh, that sounds about right coming from her.

Just kidding, I did some light grilling. Seems like a good guy. Not everyone will be Jay *hugs* - T

She's not wrong, and I know not every guy out there is going to be a crazy, psychotic asshole, but Jay didn't start out that way either.

I stare at my phone for a few minutes debating as to whether I want to text him back, before ultimately deciding to go ahead and do it. What's the harm? It's only a text.

It's all good, I kind of figured she'd cave. – Cass

LOL! Do you know all your friends that well? – C

The ones that matter. – Cass

Damn, are you saying I don't matter? – C

I'm saying we just met, so it doesn't count – Cass

Fair enough, but I bet I can make you change your mind – C

I shake my head and laugh to myself, there's no way it will ever happen. But, if he's content to try and make it happen, I suppose it will be interesting to watch him try.

Go on a date with me – C

I stare at the message, shock on my face. I imagine if people were staring at me right at this moment, they would think that someone had died rather than asked me out.

I don't think that's a good idea – Cass

It's not that I don't want to, but Jay's many threats are still very real to me and I don't want to bring anybody into my world filled of paranoia. It's one of the reasons I've stayed away from Taylor.

Why? – C

I don't know what to tell him, the truth is, I don't want to tell him anything because we don't know each other.

Because we don't know each other. You could be a serial killer, or a stalker, or who knows what – Cass

He doesn't respond for a few minutes and I use the time to shut off the television in the living room and move to my bedroom.

I have a television in my bedroom too, along with access to my security system. I hate sleeping in the silence and the dark, so I always have it on.

What kind of people do you date? I can give you character references if you need them, but I'm no serial killer or stalker. – C

PS – that's why we should go on a date – C

I laugh. He's persistent and charming, a dangerous combination.

I'll think about it. For now, I'm going to bed. Goodnight – Cass

Oh god, why did I say that.

I'll take it. Goodnight for now – C

CHAPTER SIX

Colt

It's not perfect, but it's a start. At least she's talking to me. I look around my rented condo and sigh. I have a feeling I'm going to be here for a while. I love my job, I really do, but there are times when it kind of sucks.

We're a bit of a misfit group, Red aka Tim, Chris, myself and Ike. But, despite our differences, we're a family. We've all been through too much, some more than others and some of us still trying to deal with the demons of our past.

Despite all our faults and demons, we're always there for each other. I wasn't lying when I talked to Cassie, it really is nice knowing you have someone you can trust in your corner.

We came together by chance. Ike and I met a few years back at a bar. I could tell he was looking for a fight and I was looking for someone to take home. The way he was looking that night, he was going to take down the whole bar and there was a gorgeous brunette, that I wanted to be under.

Instead of letting him get his ass kicked, I decided to step in and offer to share my brunette. I still remember how wild and crazy his eyes looked when I suggested it. I also remember how much calmer he was after he was done with her.

Ike introduced me to Chris, his brother. They're like night and day in some ways, and exactly alike in others. Ike is hot-headed and Chris is calm. I've never seen him lose his shit. But they both go through women like there's no tomorrow.

Red, he's more of a behind the scenes guy and that's what he prefers. He found us, because he needed help finding someone. Someone that he couldn't find, and he can find anything. I mean everything. He finds the most obscure shit, just to piss us off. We haven't found what he's looking for yet, but we haven't given up either. It's an ongoing project for us.

We're not a group of people you call if you want something done on the books. We don't claim to be those people. We're also not people you reach easily.

Naturally, when we get a new job, we jump right into it. But, as soon as we have down time, we all start to dig a little. Not just on our mark, but also the person who paid for the contract on the mark. So far, Cassie is reading like someone who is in hiding. We may be fighting for the wrong side this time.

I lift open my laptop, I have a bit more research to do before I'm able to sleep tonight.

CHAPTER SEVEN

Cassie

Last night might have been the best night I've had in a while, but waking up this morning, brought reality crashing down.

The first thing I do after forcing myself to wake up, is to scroll the news then check my messages.

This morning I woke up to a lot of messages.

How did it go last night? – T

I can't believe you haven't texted me back – T

You better be texting him instead of me – T

Hope you slept well – C

Good Morning (smiley face) – C

Then I got a few messages from an anonymous number.

Hope you had fun bitch.

Did you enjoy flirting?

Hope he's worth it.

Now I'm freaking out. I didn't feel anyone watching me last night. I made sure I was vigilant in my walk to and from the bar. But I must have missed something and now I'm trying to retrace my steps in my mind to see what it was I missed.

No matter how hard I think, nothing sticks out. Unless

something happened at the bar when I was talking to Colt, but I think I would have noticed if something was wrong. No matter how distracted I might have been, if there was danger, I would have noticed.

My phone buzzes again.

Are you alive? – T

Taylor always worries about me; this is what happens when I disappear and reappear. She feels like she has to take care of me. If I don't text her back, she'll come over and bang on the door until I let her in.

I'm alive. Just woke up – Cass

My phone immediately begins to ring, and I don't even have to look to know it's Taylor.

"Hi, Taylor," I answer, putting my phone on speaker.

"Why don't you answer your texts?" she asks.

"Maybe, because I was asleep?" I laugh.

"Why do you sleep so much?"

"I don't know, maybe it's because what normal people do after a night of drinking?"

I can hear her laughing.

"God, I've missed you, Cass. Where have you been, really? Why didn't you reach out to me?"

"Tay, I really am sorry, but you know things didn't end on the best terms with Jay."

"No, that's where you're wrong," she interrupts loudly. "I have no fucking idea what happened. All I know is that things ended, and you disappeared."

I sigh, "I feel like I'm apologizing a lot, but I truly am sorry. I didn't want to keep you in the dark, but I was doing what I thought was best."

"Best for who? For you or for me?" she asks.

"I…I…" I stutter, "I think for both of us."

"Bullshit, you did it to protect yourself," she says, angrily.

"Hey! You have no idea what I went through," I spit angrily.

"You're right I don't, because you shut me out!" she punches out. "Fuck this. Don't go anywhere, because I'm coming over now."

I listen to the dial tone as it fills my room and shake my head. She'll be over here in no time and I know she won't fall for any of my bullshit excuses. I just don't know if I'm ready to tell her the truth.

CHAPTER EIGHT

Colt

I don't like that I'm not able to find anything on the person that hired us.

I reach for my phone and dial Red.

"This better be fucking good," he answers, groggily.

"How much do you know about the person that hired us for this job?" I ask, getting straight to the point.

"Colt?"

"No, it's the damn, Pope," I pause. "Yes, it's Colt. Who were you expecting?"

"I don't know it's late. Give me a minute to wake up."

I wait and listen as I hear the rustling of covers and running water in the background.

"Okay, what's wrong?" he asks.

"Who hired us for this job?"

"It came across as anonymous, but I did a little digging and the person was using a fake name at an internet café. I pulled up the cameras from the café at the time we received the job and the cameras had already been wiped."

"You don't think that's a little odd?" I question, brusquely.

"Of course, I do," he says, a hint of irritation entering

his voice. "I'm not in the business of torturing people that don't deserve it. You should know me better than that."

"Sorry," I say, uncomfortably. I really do feel bad. I know he would never hurt someone innocent not after everything he's been through and what he's still going through.

"Damn right you're sorry, asshole. Anyways, as I was saying. I don't hurt innocent people and since the person who hired us went out of their way to find us and then conceal themselves, I figured we should take this job. You know in case it ended up turning into a protection detail instead. I have Ike checking out the internet café in person. I didn't want to tell you or Chris about it right now because I don't know anything yet. For all we know the information we got could be right. I'm going to assume you're calling me at this ungodly hour though, because you got the same feeling I did. Something doesn't feel right about this job."

"Yes, something about the way she was acting tonight, makes me think she was afraid of something or someone. Not only that, did you notice her ring? She kept fiddling with it all night, but never called anyone or made any attempt to reach out to a significant other. I didn't hear Taylor mention one either," I say.

"Chris mentioned the same thing," he adds, thoughtfully. "I'll check in with Ike and see if he found anything. For now, try and stay close to her. I'll have Chris shadow you in case anything happens."

"Sounds good. Thanks man."

"No problem. Night," he says, absently.

"Night."

I can tell his mind is racing now. I'm glad we're on

the same page though. At least my hunting skills haven't dulled. For now, there's nothing I can do other than wait.

I may as well sleep. I close my laptop, do a quick security check and head to the bedroom. I open my phone and quickly send a few texts to Cassie. I want to make sure she knows I'm thinking of her.

I realize as I send the texts, I'm only doing it partially because of the job. I really did have a good time tonight. So much so, that at times I almost forgot I had a job to do.

With any luck, tonight my dreams will be filled with her.

CHAPTER NINE

Cassie

She's going to be here any minute and I'm not ready for her. I quickly throw on sweats, run a quick comb through my hair and put on a pot of coffee. I'd love to just make myself a cup this morning, but I know it's not going to be one of those mornings.

I turn off the alarm and wait for inevitable, incessant, pounding at my door that is Taylor. Sure enough, as I'm mixing my coffee, I hear a banging at my door.

"I'm coming, stop your horrid noise before you wake up everyone on the block," I say, opening the door.

"You know why I'm here," she says, blowing past me.

"Please come in," I say, shutting the door behind her.

"You need to start talking woman," she says.

I watch as she grabs a mug from the cupboard and makes herself a cup a coffee and laugh.

"What?" she asks. "You know you would have just told me to make myself at home anyways, so I'm saving you the trouble," she shrugs.

I roll my eyes, "Whatever. When you're done making yourself at home, we can talk about what you want to know."

I walk over and sit on the couch and wait for her to finish raiding my kitchen.

"Spill," she says, sitting.

"What specifically are you wanting?" I ask, cautiously.

"Why'd you go all invisible on me?" she asks, plopping down next to me.

"You know Jay and I broke up," I begin cautiously.

"Duh."

"Well it wasn't a very amicable break-up," I say. Technically, that isn't a lie. I'm tip toeing around the truth. I really don't want to bring Taylor into this, especially after the texts I got this morning.

"How so?" she asks, giving me a look.

"It just didn't end well."

"Lots of things don't end well, Cass, that doesn't mean you lock yourself in your house and away from everything you know and love for over a fucking year!" she says, exasperation seeping into her voice.

"True, but this ended really poorly. I needed some time to myself. You know how long Jay and I were together. I deserve time to wallow and repair myself. I'm still not sure I'm ready to venture out."

"Cass, there is a difference in wallowing and rebuilding yourself and doing whatever you did or, are doing. What you're doing isn't healthy. You've managed to cut yourself off from everyone who cares about you and you didn't have that many people to begin with."

I sigh, "Look, I know it may seem stupid or impulsive, but I know I was, or am making the right decision. If people don't want to stick around, fine. I didn't need them in my life in the first place."

"Damn. That's fucking harsh."

I shrug, "It is what it is."

"I guess so," she looks at me, unconvinced.

I sip my coffee as she scrutinizes me and give her nothing. The last thing I need is for her to be suspicious of anything going on right now.

She stands, "I don't believe you, but I also don't believe you're going to tell me the truth either."

I go to speak, but she cuts me off, before I can even begin.

"It's fine. You'll either tell me or you won't. It really is okay. Just don't disappear on me without a heads up. Do me that courtesy, okay?"

I watch as she puts her coffee cup in the sink and walks back over to me.

"I can do that."

"Thank you," she says, hugging me. "I have to get to the bar to do some inventory. Are you coming out tonight?"

"I'm going to try to. I'll text you."

"Okay, sounds good. Have a good day."

"You too," I say, walking her to the door.

I watch as she walks away and hesitates slightly, as if she wants to stop and say something, then shakes her head and continues.

I breathe a sigh of relief and lock the door. That was too close.

CHAPTER TEN

Colt

I wake still alone and without information. I check my phone to see if I have any messages from Cassie but find none. It shows she's read my messages, but she's chosen not to get back to me yet. Not to sound too much like a girl, but it kind of sucks.

I hop in the shower, rinsing off quickly, the cold water a jolt to my system. I hear my phone ringing in the other room and race to get it. There are only a few people it could be and honestly as much as I would like for it to be Cassie, I need to hear back from Red.

Not knowing what this mission is bothers me. I don't enjoy going into things blind. If she is the mission, then I need to keep my focus and not get distracted by her. If she isn't then it's a different story. I can get close to her and protect her. Until I know the truth, I'm in limbo.

I reach my phone and see it's a number I don't know.

"Hello?" I answer, cautiously.

"Colt," a female voice, responds.

"Who is this?" I ask.

"What you don't remember the name of the woman who so kindly funneled booze to you all night and then gave you the number of her best friend?" she teases.

"Taylor?" How did you get this number?"

"I have my ways, but that's not the point."

"Okay..." I draw out. "What is the point then?"

"Cassie's hiding something from me."

"I don't see what that has to do with me, we just met last night," I reply.

"What is up with people and their bullshit today? Look Colt, if that is your name. I honestly, don't give a fuck why you came to my bar. What I do care about are your reasons for talking to my friend. I know there is more to you than what you're telling me and that's fine. But I meant what I said last night if you hurt her on purpose, I'll find you and hurt you. So, if you're here to hurt her, tell me now, so I can find someone to protect her."

I'm immediately on edge, "Why would she need someone to protect her?"

"That's not an answer," she fires back.

"Maybe it's not an answer I can give."

"Or maybe that's some bullshit."

"Maybe it is, but maybe I need more information before I can get you that information."

I can hear her sighing in the background. "I think she may be in trouble. She disappeared for a while, like a long while. As in last night was the first night, I had seen her in almost a year. Then, you randomly show up and sweet talk her. I go over this morning to figure out what the fuck is going on and she's evasive as all hell and all I can get out of her is that her break up with her ex was difficult. It's all bullshit. So, somebody needs to tell me what the fuck is going on."

I try to digest the information I've just been given.

"Are you still there? Or did you blow me off?"

"No, I'm still here. Did you know her ex?" I ask.

"Not really. I met him a few times, but whenever we hung out, Cassie was different. Quieter," she reflects.

"I don't know why I'm here right now. The reason is a bit muddy at the moment. I enjoyed my time with her last night though, probably more than I should have. What I will say is this, you've provided me with some valuable information I didn't have before."

"You know that doesn't help me," she sighs. "Can you promise me you won't hurt her?"

"Not until I know more," I pause. "I'm sorry. I truly hope it doesn't come to that. If things change, I'll let you know, but right now no."

"You realize I'm going to have to tell her, right?" she says.

"Why would you do that?"

"Because you're threatening to hurt my best friend. I'm already worried one crazy person may be trying to hurt her, I don't need a second person," she says adamantly.

"Can you give me the rest of the day before you say anything, please?"

"I'll give you until three p.m. today. If I don't hear from you by then, I'm letting her know not to trust you. Oh, and when you call me back, you better give me a damn good reason why I should trust you," she says.

I go to reply but all I hear is a dial tone.

"I'm fucked," I say, to the empty room.

I quickly dial Red and wait for him to answer, "What's up?" he says.

"We have a problem," I say.

CHAPTER ELEVEN

Cassie

I really dodged a bullet with Taylor. If she found out what really happened with Jay, she'd lose her shit. I'm just not ready to share it with her yet. One day, maybe, but today is not that day.

I can only handle one thing at a time and the next thing I need to handle is Colt. He is an unexpected addition to my life and I'm not sure why he's here now. I want to believe he's a good person who just happened to be in the right place at the right time. But, I'm not so naïve to believe that things like that happen to girls like me. Everything happens for a reason. Every action has a reaction and not all of them are good.

So, why is this man in my life, now? If he's not a good man, what could I have possibly done to deserve this? I've more than paid my dues in life. If he is good, is it possible I'm lucky enough to have something good for once?

I rub my face and sigh, "Fuck."

"Why isn't life just easy?" I say, to the empty room.

I hear the notification on my phone go off and check to see who's messaging me.

I know you're alone.

It's the anonymous number from before. I start typing out a message, but my finger hovers over the send button, wondering whether responding is the smartest idea. On the other hand, if I don't respond, I'll never know who is sending these messages and do I really want to live like this forever?

Who is this? What do you want?

Better to have some answer then no answer at all.

Why are you alone?

I read the text trying to figure out why I'm getting the message.

Who is this? I message back.

I put my phone down and move to go do something else, but my phone immediately pings.

Why does it matter? Why are you alone?

Now, I'm just getting annoyed.

Because I'm a grown ass woman.

I thought you were scared and hiding.

I freeze. There's no way it could be him. I changed my number a half a dozen times so he couldn't contact me anymore. I didn't move, but I swore I wouldn't let him take everything from me.

Jay… I message back. My entire body is so tense I feel like I could break at any second.

You wish. I'm worse than him.

I swallow as I read the messages on my phone. My heart is beating so hard and fast, it's as if it's trying to escape my chest.

I know where you are… always. I know your fears. Your friends. Your secrets.

My hands begin to shake, and the words begin to blur. I'm having a panic attack. I blink and try to slow my breathing, like I learned online.

The best part... I know your security code.

I can't help it; a small gasp escapes and I turn to find a large man standing in the doorway.

"You really should change your code more frequently."

CHAPTER TWELVE

Colt

"Wʜᴀᴛ's ᴛʜᴇ ᴘʀᴏʙʟᴇᴍ?" Rᴇᴅ ᴀsᴋs.

"Taylor just called me, and she was worried about Cassie. Not only that she's smarter than she's let on. She doesn't think I just happened upon Cassie, but she doesn't know whether I'm a friend or foe. She's given me until three today to let her know which one I am. If I give her the wrong answer, she's going to rat me out to Cassie."

"Fuck!" he yells. I hear things banging in the background.

"Uh, you okay, Red?"

"No, I'm not okay, Colt. This mission has been fucked from the moment we took it and it's not getting any easier," he sighs. "Does she know of anyone else, or is it just you she's suspicious of?"

"Just me at the moment," I say, slowly. "Why what are you thinking of?"

"We could send Chris in to distract her."

"It might work, but she's going to be leery of anyone right now. Have you heard from Ike yet?" I ask.

"No, not yet and it's starting to worry me. He should have checked in by now."

"I agree. Where is Chris?" I ask.

"He's close to you, but still hidden out of sight, in case Taylor or Cassie come by. I have been working my ass off to figure out who hired us, but I'm still blocked. The more I investigate it, the less I like it. I don't want to be on the wrong side of this Colt. I can't be on the wrong side of this," he pauses. "I really don't like that we have a deadline. See if you can get a hold of Cassie and get a feel of how she is this morning then call me back. Maybe that will help move us in the right direction."

"Will do. Give me just a few minutes and I'll call you back."

I hang up and dial Cassie. Her phone rings and rings and rings. I look down and hang up. Maybe I misdialed somehow. I redial her number and listen as the phone rings again.

I finally hear someone pick up.

"Cassie?" I ask.

"I'm sorry, Cassie can't come to the phone. She's a little tied up right now," a male voice, laughs.

I immediately jump into action, "Who is this?"

"Nobody you'll ever meet," a deep voice, responds.

"Hello? Hello?" I yell, into the non-responsive phone. "Fuck!"

I quickly dial Chris and wait for him to pick up.

"What's up man?"

"No time get over to Cassie's now! She's in trouble."

His demeanor instantly changes, "Weapons or no weapons?"

"Weapons, but she's an innocent. I heard one male for sure, could be two male suspects in there with her."

"On it. I'm assuming you're on the way."

"You know I am. Texting Red and I'm out the door."

"See you there," he says, hanging up.

Someone at Cassie's. Don't know more. Will let you know when I do – C

As I'm getting into the car, I get a simple text back.

Fuck.

CHAPTER THIRTEEN

Cassie

"Who are you?" I ask, stepping backwards.

"Let's say, I'm an acquaintance of Jay's," he grins, stepping forward.

"What type of acquaintance?" I stutter. I want to be brave and strong in this moment, but I know this isn't going to go well.

"Not the kind you want," he says, taking another step forward.

"Why are you here?"

"You know why. It's time to stop with this bullshit game and come home."

"I am home," I say, defiantly.

He laughs, "No wonder Jay likes you; you've got some sass in you. But you and I both know that's not what I mean. He gets what he wants, and he wants you."

"I'm not a toy."

"You're whatever he wants you to be."

"No, I'm whatever I want to be. He and I are no longer together. He does not get a say in my life."

He steps right in front of me and grabs my arm, "He owns you until he says otherwise and as of this moment, he still wants you, though I can't understand why."

"Let go of me!" I yell, struggling to pull my arm away.

He merely smirks at my futile attempt of an escape and twists my arm behind my back.

I cry out in pain and use my other arm to punch him.

"I'm not going anywhere; you can tell him to go fuck himself," I groan.

"You're going, even if that means I end up carrying your unconscious body out of here myself."

I continue my struggle and feel the strain against my shoulder and arm.

"Fuck him and fuck you too!"

With that smart remark, he knocks me down to my knees and pushes me face first onto the ground.

"Oh, I'm sure he can arrange for that, but first I've got to get you to him."

He kneels pushing his knee into my back. I struggle to catch my breath and escape him, but I can't. I hear my phone begin to ring and my hope soars.

"Aw, don't get your hopes up yet, sweetheart, you're not going anywhere."

I hear rustling and then I feel a thick strap being wrapped around my wrists and arms.

I can't hear who's on the other end of the phone, all I can hear is what he's saying.

"I'm sorry, Cassie can't come to the phone. She's a little tied up right now," he laughs.

There's a pause then he says, "Nobody you'll ever meet."

The next thing I know he's leaning down and stroking my hair.

"Ah, I'm sorry we won't have enough time to finish this today, but I'll be watching, and I'll be back. For now, why don't you take a little nap until your cavalry arrives?"

Then everything goes black.

CHAPTER FOURTEEN

Colt

Fuck! I can't drive fast enough to get to her. Should I know where she lives, no, but do we do our homework? Yes. In any other circumstance I might feel bad, but right now, I'm grateful for the detail we put into our background searches.

I dial Taylor back and wait for her to answer.

"That was fast," she answers.

"Circumstances have changed. Wait for my call and be ready. I'm one of the good guys," I bite out.

"What do you mean circumstances have changed?"

"I'll tell you after. I don't need you charging into an already dangerous situation and making it worse. Got it?"

"Not really. I don't like taking orders, so there better be a damn good reason why you're talking to me like this."

"There is," I say, hanging up the phone.

I tap my fingers against the steering wheel as I bob and weave through traffic, fighting to get to a woman I barely know, but already feel connected to. I'm trusting my gut on this one. She is not the enemy, but whoever hired us, is.

I pull into the parking lot of Cassie's place and run. I can see the door to her place is open even before I make it there. I slow my steps slightly and have my weapon ready. I edge along the wall, listening for sounds of distress or aggression.

"Shh, I've got you now. Don't be afraid," a male voice, soothes.

My brow furrows, I tilt my head closer to the door trying to get a better angle.

"I'm a friend of Colt's, you don't have to be afraid. We're going to get you fixed up."

I hear squealing tires and my head jerks behind me to see Chris pulling in. I immediately turn back towards the door and nudge it.

"Who's in there?" I call out.

"It's Ike, you ass! Get in here."

"Ike?" I ask, bursting through the door. "What are you doing here? Aren't you supposed to be checking out surveillance?"

"I was. I was on my way back to check in with Red, when he called me to see where I was. He told me what happened, and I came here instead. I got here about five minutes ago. She just regained consciousnesses about a minute and a half ago," he says.

I look down and notice he's got her head cradled between her thighs.

"Hey, Cassie. I'd ask how you're doing, but you don't look so great," I say softly, kneeling.

She coughs then laughs. "Thanks, appreciate that." She pauses, breathing heavily, "Who are you?"

Chris bursts through the door gun raised.

"We're good man," I say.

He lowers his weapon, "Good. Hey, Ike."

"Hey, man. Can you do a quick sweep of the place?"

Chris nods and walks down the hall.

She lifts her arm and taps my knee and raises her eyebrows. I can hear sirens in the background and know we don't have a lot of time left.

"I'll fill you in when you're safe."

I watch as paramedics fill the room and step out of the way. I listen as they talk to her in hushed tones and then lift her.

"One of you can ride with us if you'd like," one of the paramedics say.

"Ike will you go with her, please?" I ask. "I'll meet up with you in a little bit."

He nods.

I step forward and reach out to grab her hand before they run off with her. "I promise, I'll tell you as much as I can when I get there. For now, Ike will keep you safe."

"Okay," she whispers.

I step back and watch as they roll her out of the house.

"You okay, man?" Chris asks, stepping out from the hallway.

"No, not at all. We got hired to do a job, but someone else decided to step in and do it anyway? It doesn't make sense."

I reach for my phone, but Chris clears his throat loudly and shakes his head. I give him a 'what the fuck' look.

"Yeah, I know. It looks like a standard break-in though. Tough luck for your girl," he says, calmly, walking towards the door.

"Why don't we grab her some flowers and meet them at the hospital?"

"Okay," I say, slightly confused.

We walk outside and Chris closes the door behind us. He makes a slight movement with his hand and I know not to say anything yet.

"That place is bugged the fuck out," Chris says, slamming the car door.

"Are you serious?" I ask.

"Yeah, voice and video. I can't tell how long they've been there, but she's being watched. Which means we're probably being watched right now. So, move, we can call Red on the drive."

"What the fuck have we stumbled onto?" I ask.

"No clue, but we're going to find out," he says.

CHAPTER FIFTEEN

Cassie

I'm running in a dark space. There's no light and I can't find my way out. But I can hear Jay's voice taunting me.

"I can find you anywhere Cassie girl, don't forget it," the voice taunts.

"Shut up, Jay!" I yell into the abyss.

I hear laughter echo around me and crumble to the ground. It's his voice. Why is it always his voice?

I remember what happened the day he left. When I finally said enough was enough. Even in this dark space it makes me cringe.

It wasn't always this way though. We had known each other since grade school. Known may be a bit of an overstatement. We were aware of each other in grade school. Jay was the kind of person who everyone loved. He had a magnetic personality from a young age. Teachers, parents and other students were just drawn to him.

I was fascinated by him, but I saw something in his eyes that scared me. My parents told me I was being silly and there was nothing to be afraid of. Looking back on it, I was right, and she was wrong.

I was safe from Jay for several years. I was just the quiet girl in the corner who nobody paid attention too. I was fine with that, then one day everything changed. It was the day Jay said hello to me.

From the moment he acknowledged me, I was a someone. Girls wanted to be my friend, they invited me to their sleepovers and birthday parties. The boys protected me from bullies. It was all nice, but it all came with a price.

It wasn't until high school that Jay made his move on me. He began to court my family as he courted me. I was never sold on him, but my family fell in love with him. They thought he was sweet, and they thought it was sweeter he was taking the time to meet them.

When he finally asked me out, I felt as if I couldn't say no. He asked me to a movie in front of my parents and I remember looking back at their faces and they looked so hopeful. So, I said yes.

My life was never the same after that day. At first, we just went on small dates. I wasn't necessarily enjoying myself, but I figured I could get out of it any time I wanted. Then a year passed, and he started getting me small gifts. I tried to return them, but my mother said it would be rude.

It was then I realized they were completely under his spell. I knew I wouldn't have my parents support when it came to Jay. I thought if I could get away to college then I could get away from him for good.

I threw myself into school, getting the best grades I could. I wanted to go to a school as far from home as possible and I made it happen. I left my parents and Jay behind and moved across the country.

At least I thought I did. That was the first time I realized no matter how far I went; I couldn't escape him.

I was on my own for months enjoying life, meeting friends and finally relaxing. Then one day he showed up in a limo with a dozen roses in front of the building of one of my classes. So, as soon as my lecture was letting out, there he was with this grand gesture of romance. I froze and all the girls gave me this look of envy. I have no idea how he found out my class schedule but looking back nothing surprises me anymore.

I can't remember the exact words he said to me that day, but I remember he walked up to me with such confidence and he talked about how much he missed me. Then he swept me into his arms, and I was lost.

Somehow, he had found me and trapped me again, even though it was all the way across the country. I fought him for years. In public he was the perfect gentleman, in private I hid from him as much as possible.

I only went out in public with him if I had to. Otherwise, I avoided him at all costs. Things didn't go well if we were alone together. He was not, is not, a nice man. I was on the receiving end of his fists more times than I care to remember.

Then, the day came I knew I had to end things. The day he proposed to me. I remember he got down on one knee in front of his security personnel, with the most predatory smile and asked me to be his wife. I was in shock. I knew if I said yes, I wouldn't live long. So, I did the only thing I possibly could. I told him no and to get the fuck out of my house.

I watched his face go from shock to pure fury. I felt the anger from him and his security team, but I made sure to keep myself as close to the door as possible. I wanted an exit and I wanted to make sure people could hear me if I needed to scream.

I opened the door as he stood and walked towards me. I wanted to make sure none of them were able to touch me without someone seeing. I waited for him to gather his things and I kept a close watch on all his men as they watched me.

His parting words will always scare me and now I know they're true. He will always come for me and there's nothing I can do.

"Thank you for the lovely trip down memory lane," Jay laughs.

"Why are you doing this?" I cry out.

"How many times do I have to tell you? You're mine. You will always be mine. You've been mine since the day I laid eyes on you in grade school and what I want, I get."

"I'm not a prize, Jay! I've always told you that. Go find someone who wants that."

I begin to cry. I need to find a way out of here. Instead of wallowing, I force myself up and run.

I can hear faint noises and my name being said. All I can do is run to it.

"You can run all you want, but I'll find you," he laughs. "They'll never be able to save you and protect you."

His voice taunts me as I run faster and faster to the people calling my name. I will escape him this time.

My eyes jerk open, "No!"

CHAPTER SIXTEEN

Colt

"Yeah, so her house is covered in bugs," Chris says.

"What do you mean covered in bugs?" Red asks, loudly through the speaker.

"Exactly what he said, there's video and sound surveillance. Who knows how long she's been watched? She can't go back to that house," I say, calmly.

"You're right, she can't. Also, we need to talk about who hired us. I think I have a hit on the person who did it. Ike wasn't able to get anything from the tapes but got some verbal confirmation of an individual that might be of interest to us."

"I'm sure Colt will let her stay with him," Chris offers.

I flip him off, "Yes, she can stay with me."

"Good. Call me as soon as you have her and you're out of the hospital. Also, how the fuck did Taylor get my number?" he asks, incredulously.

"Damn, she's a sneaky one. She jacked either mine or Chris' phone. Just like she did to Cassie's phone," I say.

"Wow, I really want to meet this woman now. She called and yelled at me."

Chris and I both start laughing, "Damn, you haven't

even met her, and she's got you tied up in knots."

"She yelled at me, she said if we were supposed to be taking care of Cassie, we were doing a piss poor job and if we didn't step up she was going to hunt down our whole team and kick our asses personally," he says, shock in his voice.

"Holy fuck," Chris says.

"Damn, there is more to that woman than she lets on," I say.

"No shit. You think I didn't immediately realize that? I have one miniscule problem though."

"What?" Chris asks.

"I only have her first name!" He yells, "Yet somehow, she has all this information about me and better yet, she knows about us. The only person she hasn't mentioned yet, is Ike. I'd like to keep at least one person in our group a secret."

"Uh, yeah about that. So, um, Ike is with Cassie now. If Taylor doesn't know about Ike yet, she will soon."

"Mother fucker! How has one job fucked up everything we've done? One job! We've been fine for years and now, one job might fuck everything up," he says, annoyed.

"Look, we don't know she's out to ruin us. She could just be really protective of Cassie," I say.

"Since when does that ever work out for us," he says.

"Okay, fine, but still, these are just two women who are friends. I can't imagine Taylor is trying anything suspicious."

"Colt, when you're wrong, can I hit you?" Red asks.

"When I'm right, can I hit you?" I ask.

"Deal," he says.

"Deal," I agree.

"Colt just pulled into the parking lot of the hospital. We'll go check on Cassie and get her out of there as soon as possible. Then I'll call you when we're all back at my place."

I hang up and shake my head.

"Clusterfuck," I say.

"Agreed," he say, getting out of the car.

CHAPTER SEVENTEEN

Cassie

"You are very big," I say, to the large man looking down at me.

He laughs and a deep robust sound fills the room, making me smile.

"Why are you smiling?" he asks.

"I honestly don't know. I didn't think your laugh would sound like that. It surprised me," I say, smiling.

"I'll take that as a compliment," he grins. "Yes, I am big, but I need to be for my line of work."

"What is it that you do? Wait, better first question. What's your name?"

"I feel as if I should be concerned by the fact that you're not more worried with the fact you're sitting in a hospital bed right now, but we'll get back to that in a minute. For now, I'm Ike."

"Hi, Ike! I'm Cassie and yeah, you'd think I'd be worried about this, but it's not my first time here. I'm just not sure I remember the trip here this time," I pause. "To be fair, also not a first for me."

I watch Ike's face go slack and then hear the door open.

"Who's that?" I ask cheerfully.

"No, you should not be that cheerful about this," he scolds.

"Cheerful about what?" Colt asks.

I watch as Colt and the guy from the bar walk in.

"Ah, so you all know each other?"

They all give each other a look and Chris says, "Yes."

"Go back to what you were saying about the cheerful thing. I told you, I would tell you as much as I could about us as I would, but not here."

The door opens again.

"Are you back again, Cassie?" a voice asks.

"Again?" the men ask in unison.

"Hi, Doctor S. How have you been?" I ask, cheerfully.

"It's been a while. Longer than the last time, so you must have found a safe spot like we talked about," he says.

He looks around the room, "Or maybe you hired security, which is also a good idea."

"No, this is actually a new development," I shrug.

"Interesting," he pauses. "Do you want to discuss this in front of them?"

I look around the room, "I feel like they're either going to figure it out or make me tell them, so they may as well hear it now."

"Gentleman, it seems she's given you permission to stay. However, I will let you know now this is her decision. Should she decide at any point that she does not want you in here, you will leave immediately," the doctor says, as he stares us down.

"Understood," they say.

He turns back to me, "So, what did you do?"

"What did you mean?" I ask.

"I guess it's a two-part question. How did you hurt yourself and how did you manage to keep away so long this time?"

"I finally said no," I say.

He looks at me shocked, "You said, no?"

"I know, I couldn't believe it either. I just knew if I didn't say something then, the next time I was coming back here was going to be in a body bag. Unfortunately, he made good on his psychotic last words, which is how I ended up here today. He always said nobody told him no. To be fair, today it wasn't him, but it was one of his people. If I know him, it was one of his security people that he sent after me. You know the deal."

He sighs, "I do. I mean I'm glad you said something, but this is one of the more serious visits. You haven't had a broken bone in quite some time. Lately, I've been treating you for massive bruising and some bruised and cracked ribs. This is bad, I can't say conclusively, but I'd guess you have a concussion. Your arm was torn out of socket and your wrist is broken. You may have some tendons torn in your shoulder, but I can't tell what's new and what's old damage. So, I'm going to cast up your wrist and keep you in sling until the cast comes off. You'll need to come back for another set of images on that shoulder though."

I keep my eyes firmly planted on the doctor and try to avoid the three sets of eyes that are staring back at me.

"I'd also assume your ribs are bruised if not broken. You've been gone for a while, but not long enough for the last set to heal."

"Understood. How long do I have to be here?" I ask.

"Always in such a hurry to leave," he chides.

"Well, I never liked hospitals. Plus, the longer I was away the longer he felt the need to make things up to me. I was never in the mood, so, it really was just a vicious circle."

"Can I trust you all will be there to take care of her?" he asks the group.

"Where is my friend?" I hear from the hallway.

We all look to the door.

"I'm pretty sure that's Taylor. Someone may want to get her, before she ruins everyone's day."

Chris peeks his head out the door and waves.

"Cassie? Cassie?" I hear.

I watch as she walks in the room and then looks around.

"What the fuck is going on?" she demands.

"Let me finish first, then you can discuss what you need to discuss," the doctor says.

She nods.

"As I was saying, will one of you be able to take care of her at least for a week?"

"Yes, we all will," Colt says.

"Then give me just a minute to write everything up. Then, I'll cast you up myself and you should be able to leave within the hour. Are you sure you don't want me to report this?" he asks.

I reach out and grab his arm, "Please. Promise me you won't. He's too dangerous and you've done too much for me. I can't promise you'll be safe," I finish softly.

He pats my hand, "Okay, I have to be sure. But if you ever change my mind, I keep a very secret stash of all our encounters."

I smile, "Thank you."

"Alright, have your conversation. I'll be back shortly.

"So, what the fuck is going on?" Taylor asks.

Colt clears his throat, "Ike, Chris, Red and I are an elite group of people who you hire when you want something done. Something that you don't necessarily want done on the books. Well, an anonymous person hired us to take out Cassie."

"Uh, excuse me," Taylor interrupts. "Take out? Can you please be more specific?"

"Kill," Ike states.

"Are you freaking kidding me?" she whispers, angrily.

She glares at Colt, "You told me you were a good guy." She pokes him in the chest.

"Ouch!" he says, rubbing his chest. "I am the good guy."

I watch the interaction from bed slightly amused, waiting for the rest of the story.

"Look, we are the good guys. We took the job because we were paid to take the job. Red started looking into who paid us shortly after we took the job and sent Ike to investigate," Colt says.

"Red doesn't take jobs that he thinks are shady. He has been doing some digging and he sent me to do some in person investigating after we took the job, which doesn't happen very often. Mainly because we don't have this type of problem," Ike says. "Basically, what we have is an anonymous dick who was too good at computers. I managed to get a really vague in-person description of the person who was at the café when they made the reservation, but that's about it."

"Red said he had something but, he didn't want to discuss it until we were all together," Chris adds.

"But, when you called and voiced your concerns, it just added to my already suspicious feelings about this job. I didn't believe Cassie was capable of committing any of the heinous acts the person who hired us accused her of," Colt says.

"Wait, what did they accuse me of?" I inquire.

"Murder and torture," Ike states.

My jaw drops, "You thought I could be capable of that?"

"It was before any of us knew you," Colt says, apologetically.

"You have to understand we've met some really horrible people in our line of work. Some of whom seem truly kind and caring. But, in the end they aren't. We had to at least check you out," Chris says.

"We've had issues in the past a disgruntled ex or someone who's been holding a grudge against our mark, takes out a misguided hit on an innocent person. Our mission then changes from murder to protection. We then track down who hired us and gently nudge the authorities in the direction of that person. Then go on our way. The benefactor of this mission has been overly aggressive." Colt says.

"That means your benefactor, as you lovingly called him, wants something. He either wants the job done quicker. Or he wants to the pin the job on you guys," Taylor murmurs aloud.

I watch as all eyes swing to Taylor's face. Including

mine.

"Um, care to run that by us again?" Ike says.

"Oh, come on you're not stupid enough to not see it," she chides.

I watch as Taylor rubs her forehead. "I'm really going to throw it all away for this," she mumbles.

"Throw what away," I ask curiously.

She walks over to me and puts her hands on mine. "Before I say what I'm about to say, I need you to understand something. What I'm about to say changes nothing about our friendship. I need you to understand that. Our friendship was real."

"Okay," I say, slowly.

I can see the boys giving each other a look behind Taylor's back.

"I'm undercover, FBI and I was assigned to watch and protect you," she says, warily.

"Whoa." "Damn." "Fuck." The boys say in unison.

I clear my throat. "I think we need to table this conversation until we're somewhere safe. Somewhere, where nobody can be listening. I realize it may never be completely safe to talk anywhere but it'll at least be safer than here. I was supposed to have my questions answered and now I somehow have more questions than before."

"Where are we going?" Taylor asks.

"My place," Colt says.

CHAPTER EIGHTEEN

Colt

It was easily one of the most uncomfortable drives I've ever been a part of. As soon as we pulled into my parking area, everybody leapt out of the vehicle.

The tension was thick between all of us. Cassie was processing what Taylor had said. We were all processing what Taylor had said and what it meant for us. Plus, Cassie has to process what we had told her. Cassie really has the shit end of this deal.

We walk into my condo and I run a quick diagnostic and give the all clear.

"We're good to talk. There's nothing here," I say.

"I'll get Red on the phone," Ike says.

"Can I talk to you a minute, Cassie? Please?" I ask, holding out my hand to her.

She nods and takes my hand.

"We'll be right back," I call over my shoulder.

I lead her back to my bedroom and shut the door behind us. "Look, I want to apologize for everything."

"There's nothing to apologize for. You were doing your job," she says.

"Yes, but still, I enjoyed our time at the bar and that

wasn't planned."

"Oh, you didn't think you'd enjoy your time with me," she teases.

"You've got jokes now?" I smile, placing my hand on her hip.

She grins and looks up and down, "Hey, if you can't smile through all of this, what the fuck else are you going to do?"

"You fucking light up when you smile. Did you know that?"

I watch as a light blush creeps up her cheeks and she dips her head. I grip her waist tighter and use my other hand to nudge her head back up.

Her brown eyes are shimmering with emotion, something I've never experienced with any other woman.

I lean down and brush my lips softly across hers. I can feel her surprise as my lips graze her, the sudden gasp her body makes. As I pull away, her eyes follow mine. I feel as her hand tentatively travels up my chest to my face and pulls it back down to her face for another kiss.

Her hand snakes into my hair as my lips dance across hers. My arms clutch her, afraid someone will take her away from me. She's mine. She may not know it yet, but she's my forever.

I pull away, ending the best kiss of my life, and lay my forehead against hers. If I don't stop now, I'm going to have a hard time stopping at all.

She smiles, "I understand. Thank you for this."

"What do you mean?"

She shrugs and tries to pull away.

"I did this because I didn't want to waste another minute not kissing you. I should have kissed you that night, but things were still up in the air. I didn't kiss you out of pity, if that's what you're thinking. I kissed you because I wanted to."

She nods, smiling.

"Good." I give her a quick kiss and grab her hand. "Now, let's get back out there, before they kill each other."

CHAPTER NINETEEN

Cassie

I'm barely paying attention to what Colt is saying to me. I'm still reeling from that kiss. I thought my body lit up from a touch, well, it went full on crazy for a kiss. His lips are so soft and sent tingles through my entire body. I feel like I'm visibly shaking.

The moment his lips brushed mine, I was done. Nobody will ever be able to compare to that.

I realize I should be more concerned about the fact that I was assaulted tonight and that I'm in danger. The fact that nobody around me is who they say they are and that there is a good chance I won't make it through this, would put most normal people into a tailspin.

This is just life for me. I've come to expect the unexpected, which I suppose makes it expected. I will say the Taylor thing has thrown me off my game, but I stopped thinking about everything the moment his lips touched mine.

As we walk back into the living room everyone's eyes immediately drop to our clasped hands and I try to discreetly pull mine from his. Instead of allowing me to pull away, he clutches it tighter.

"I told you I liked her for real. This isn't for the job. It isn't because someone told me to do it, it's because I wanted to do it. Does anyone have a problem with that?" Colt asks, looking around the room.

There are murmurs, but nothing is said.

He lifts my hand to his lips and kisses it. "There, now if you want to let go you can, but it's because you want to, not because it was weird."

I smile, "At least you get an idea of what I'm thinking already."

"Very true," he grins.

"Are we done with the mushy shit now?" a voice on the phone asks. "No offense, Cassie.

"None taken. I don't think," I say. "By the way who are you?"

"I'm Red," the voice says.

"Ahh, so you're Red," Taylor says.

"You must be Taylor," he pauses. "You're awful nosy Taylor, is there anything you want to tell us?" Red asks.

"They already know I'm FBI and I'm undercover. Sorry to ruin your big reveal," she taunts.

I watch as the guys hold back a laugh.

"Actually, I didn't know that yet. Your team did a good job covering you," he says.

She scoffs, "My team? My team abandoned me about six months ago. I covered my tracks on my own, from you, from them, from everyone."

"Son-of-a-bitch," Red says.

"Then why did you stay with me?" I ask her.

"I told you, I'm your friend and I'm not going anywhere.

Yes, my job was to protect you, but I became your friend and your friendship meant more to me and *you* meant more to me than the job did. So, when you disappeared for months on end without any word to anyone. My bosses back at Quantico, said you were a dead end and we needed to move on. I didn't believe that was true. I knew if you were gone, there was a reason for it. So, I stayed," she says, matter-of-factly.

"Uh, Taylor, we've all had our fair share of interactions with the government. You don't just tell them to fuck off and hope for the best," Ike says.

"Yeah, I got the impression they weren't pleased with me staying, but I also got the feeling they weren't telling me something while I was here," she shrugs.

"What do you mean?" Red asks.

"I'd walk into a briefing a few minutes early and find the other Agents, whispering to one another, but the minute they saw me, they'd stop. From then on, I didn't let them know everything. I wasn't sure whose side everybody was on anymore, but I knew whose side I was on."

She steps to me and grabs my good hand. "I'm so sorry I couldn't be there for you the way you needed me to be there for you. But, please let me be there for you now. Please let me help you guys out and get this bastard."

I nod, a bit shell-shocked by everything she's told me, and she wraps me in a hug.

"I'm so sorry, for everything," she whispers.

"It's okay, really, you were just doing what you had to do," I say quietly.

"I hate to interrupt what I assume is a beautiful moment,

but I really need to know everything now. From everyone. This way we can compare notes," Red says, apologetically.

"It's okay, Red. I get it really." I sigh, sitting down. "I won't bore you with how far it went back, but I'll tell you this. I tried to escape across the country when I went to college and it didn't work. Jay always found me. From a young age, he always had everything he wanted no matter what it cost. When I declined his proposal and sent him away, I don't know what changed about him with his fascination with me. He had women lining up to be with him, he didn't need me."

"That was the problem, Cassie. Don't you see it?" Chris asks, softly.

"You were the one person who said no," Colt finishes.

"Well, that makes sense. I did repeatedly turn him down," I reflect.

"Do you know what he did for a living?" Red asks.

"I don't know for certain," I begin, "But, I think it had to do with selling women for money."

"Why do you think it had to do with that?" Taylor asks.

"This was before any of you came into the picture. I was getting coffee one morning at a little café across from an apartment at my college campus, right before he came back for me and someone from the FBI joined me at my table. He asked me if I knew anything about my boyfriend's affairs. I told him I didn't have a boyfriend and I had no idea what they were talking about. When I got up to leave, he grabbed my arm and warned me."

"What did he say?" Colt asks, leaning forward.

"He said, I needed to watch my back and I shouldn't

trust anybody."

I watch everyone look around warily and shrug, "I don't know, I'd say he was probably right."

CHAPTER TWENTY

Colt

"Hey don't say that," I order.

"Why shouldn't I?" Cassie snaps. "You've all lied to me. Every single person in this room. I'm just here trying to protect myself and you are all just making it so much worse. Why? Because, you're lying to me!"

She takes a deep breath and continues, "Do you want to know why I've been so calm through all of this bullshit? It's easy. It's because I've been through it before. It's never the same, but it's always some version of this. Although, never with this many people and never this many people on my side," she waves her good hand. "But that isn't the point. My point is he always finds me. He always tries to force the point that I'm his, and I always tell him I'm not. I will not let him drag me down with him. Granted this was one of the rougher times, but I made it out. I know he still controls my life, because I fear him. But I know for the next few months I'll have peace, because he'll be satisfied with whatever the big ogre who came here tells him."

"Cassie, I really don't want to be the person to break this to you, but it's not the same this time. You need to understand that," Ike begins gently.

"Jay hired us to kill you," Red continues. "Then in case we failed or as insurance, who knows, he had someone else come and try to kill you. Do you really think that sounds like a person who is going to back off?" he asks.

I watch as she swallows nervously, "Probably not."

"We aren't trying to scare you; we just want you to see the facts. He's coming for you this time and I don't think he's going to let go," I murmur.

"I need to think," she says, walking away. We all watch as she walks down the hall and then hear a door shut.

"You can go after her in a minute, Colt, but you all need to hear this first," Red sighs. "The person who hired us is a shell. A complete fake. But, it's a good fake, I mean, it goes back to grade school. So, whoever created it, gave this person a life, just in case we decided to dig a little deeper. I just kept digging until there was nothing left to dig."

"So, what? You're thinking Jay, is the person that hired you?" Taylor asks.

"I'm guessing him or one of his lackeys, so he can say he has plausible deniability if anything were to ever come back to him," Chris adds.

I nod in agreement.

"Okay, so how do we get this asshole?" she demands.

"We don't. At least not tonight. It's been a long ass day and I for one need to sleep. So, everyone get some rest and meet back up in the morning," Red yawns.

"Sounds good to me, see you all then," Chris says.

I let everyone out, sending them off with pleasantries, but thinking of the woman, who I hope is waiting for me in my bedroom.

CHAPTER TWENTY-ONE

Cassie

"Why do you always do this to yourself?" I mumble to myself, as I pace nervously around Colt's room. "You can do this. You've done it before, and you can do it again."

I spin myself in circles, clenching and unclenching my good hand as I replay everything that's happened. Trying to rationalize everything and concluding, I can't.

"Giving yourself a pep talk?" a soft voice asks, behind me.

I jump, "Holy, fucking shit! For a big guy, you walk pretty damn quietly."

I turn clutching my chest to find a smiling Colt.

"Ugh, wipe the smile off your face, you're too cute when you do that and I need to be mad at you, at least for a minute."

"I'm not here to hurt you," he says.

"Not anymore," I mumble.

I watch his face twitch, the only sign I've hurt him and sigh. "I'm sorry, you don't deserve that."

"No, I do. I just hate hearing you say it," he says, sadly.

I sit on the edge of the bed and he kneels in front of me.

"I can't imagine what must be going through your

head right now. Honestly, we've thrown a lot at you. I need you to know I'll do anything to protect you. We will do anything to protect you. I can't speak for Taylor, because I don't know her. I do know Red, Ike and Chris and when someone wrongs someone we care about we'll go to the ends of the earth to make things right."

I look into his eyes and know he isn't lying to me. I know a liar. I've been with one, but he isn't. I believe if he was going to kill me, he would just do it.

I bend slightly and kiss him. I'm not one for making the first move. I'm too awkward and shy, I think Jay has a lot to do with that, but it feels right. It's just a brush of lips, but for a moment it's all that matters, and everything fades away.

I pull back and blush, looking down at my lap.

"Sorry," I murmur.

"For what?"

"Kissing you like that."

"Don't ever apologize for kissing me. If you want to kiss me, you kiss me."

"Okay," I smile.

I look up to find his eyes burning with desire.

"Fuck it," he says, lifting himself up slightly, bracing himself against the bed.

"Fuck what?" I tease.

He leans in and kisses me with a fire I've never felt before. My hand grips his shirt as he gently lifts and drops me backwards.

"God, you're fucking beautiful," he marvels, leaning over me.

"Stop. You're going to give me a complex."

"Damn and cheeky, when you want to be, too."

I laugh, "I guess I am."

"Well, let's see if I can work some of that cheekiness out of you."

He doesn't give me time to answer instead he nudges my head to the side, softly kissing my neck.

"If this hurts at any time," he pauses between kisses, "let me know."

"If you stop kissing me one more time, I'm going to show you where it really hurts."

He laughs, and carefully removes my tank top as to not jostle my arm before taking my breast in his hand, kneading it gently.

I moan softly as he takes a nipple in his mouth and arch my back slightly.

"None of that," he chides.

"But it feels good," I whine.

He chuckles, "I know but you can't hurt yourself more."

"I promise to tell you if it hurts."

"Right now, if you could please go back to doing what you were doing, I'd really appreciate it."

I try to look up at him with my cutest eyes and it must work, because he sighs and takes off my pants. I try not to rejoice yet, otherwise he might stop.

Then he reciprocates and takes off his pants. I lift my head just a little bit and bite my lip as I watch the fabric slide down his skin.

"I wanted to go slow, but I don't think you're going to give me that opportunity right now. So, I'm going to wear you out first then maybe I can go back and take my time the second time around."

He slides his hands up my thighs squeezing them gently as he goes. He drags his fingers softly up and down my legs until I'm squirming with need.

"Please Colt, you're killing me here. Do something."

He grins, "Are you sure?"

"Yes, I'm sure."

I watch as he strokes himself slowly as he reaches for a condom from his discarded pants. I watch in fascination as he slowly roles the condom over his long, thick cock. He places one hand by my head and uses the other to guide himself into me.

"Holy shit, you're wet."

"Yeah, it's been a while," I say, embarrassed.

"There is nothing to be embarrassed about, Cassie. That is fucking hot as hell for me. It means I really do it for you," he says, teasing me dipping the tip of his cock in and out of me.

"You do, you really do. Please no more teasing, just give it to me."

He leans over, kissing me as he pushes himself fully inside of me. I involuntarily buck at the fullness of him. Jerking my head back, panting heavily.

"Holy fuck," I moan.

"Don't move," he grunts. "You're so fucking tight; I don't know how long I'll be able to last like this."

"There's always round two," I pant, rolling my hips.

He grins and with that begins making my body feel things it never has before. I know my fingers are leaving marks in his arm, but there is something about the way he is moving that is making me fly high.

I shut my eyes and just feel. I feel the way his legs rub against mine each time he enters me. Feel the way his muscles in his arm tighten as he fights to keep his weight off me. Feel his breath against my face as he watches me. Feel the way he fills and completes me with every thrust, moan and groan. It's too much as I open my eyes to his stare and clench tightly around him and cum. As I squeeze him tightly, he groans and empties himself into me.

I know there's no going back now. Whatever I had before, whatever I thought I may have had in the past, is nothing to what I just experienced with Colt.

He pulls out and cleans himself off before bringing out a rag to gently wash me off.

"You don't have to do that," I say.

"I know, I want to though."

"Thank you."

"You're welcome, now come up here to the proper side of the bed and lay with me a bit. We've got some time before round two."

"What you can't go right away?" I tease.

"Minx! Get up here."

I smile, scooting up the bed and into his arms.

CHAPTER TWENTY-TWO

Colt

I smile at the sleeping woman in my arms. We managed to get a second and a third round in before she finally passed out. I don't know who is out to hurt her, but I'm going to find out.

I slip gently from her grasp to use the bathroom and grab a drink from the kitchen. I bring one back for her, so she'll have something in the morning and place it on the nightstand next to her.

I grab my phone to do a quick check of my messages to see if anything has happened and find a missed call and text from Taylor.

Call me when you get this. Found something big – Taylor

I don't want to wake her up, so I text her back.

What did you find? – Colt

Before I can put the phone down, it buzzes back.

HUGE. Think I finally found Jay. Think you can meet me? – Taylor

I look at the sleeping woman next to me and go out to the living room and dial Taylor.

"Are you serious?" I ask, as soon as she picks up.

"Yes! I put out tracers on certain words or phrases, so

if they were searched, I might get a hit. A lot of the times, it was nothing. Sometimes I got there, and the surveillance had been messed with. But this just happened like an hour ago. If we move fast, we can still get him," she says, excitedly.

"What about Cassie?" I ask, worriedly.

"Let her sleep, we'll be back before our morning get together. Let's go get this bastard."

"Alright, where are you now?" I ask.

"I'm at the bar."

"I'll be there in twenty," I say hanging up the phone.

I run back to the bedroom, kiss Cassie on the forehead and head out the door. I told her I would protect her, and I will.

CHAPTER TWENTY-THREE

Cassie

I open my eyes and stretch as best I can. I feel sore in the best way and the worst way at the same time. I'm not sure how it's possible, but my soreness is equaling each other out.

I look over to find the bed empty, but a glass of water sitting on the nightstand beside me.

I want to call out for Colt, but every instinct inside me is telling me to be quiet. I slip out of bed and grab my shirt and pants. I try and put them on as best I can, but my shoulder is hurting more today than it did yesterday and I end up letting out a small cry.

"Cassie? Are you okay?" a male voice asks.

"Who's there?" I tremble. I look around for any type of weapon but see none.

"It's Chris, can I come in?"

"I'll be out in a second, I'm fine, just trying to put on some clothes."

"Um, awkward question, but is Colt in there?" he whispers, loudly.

My head jerks up and I go to the door and open it a crack. "No, he isn't. He isn't with you?"

He shakes his head and motions to let him in. Colt said he would trust the guys with anything, so I let him in.

"Look, last night we got an emergency ping from his phone. Do you know what happened?"

"What do you mean, emergency ping? No, we were here in bed together and then I fell asleep and when I woke up, he was gone."

"How much do you know about Taylor?" he asks, cautiously.

"Um," I start thinking back, "I don't think she's lived here very long, but she manages the bar." I keep thinking back to our conversations, "I don't think I know anything other than the superficial information about her. I never met her family and she never talked about them. She said they weren't close, so I didn't want to pry." I look at his face, "Why?"

"Last night he got a text from her about Jay and then he called her. We don't know what they talked about, but we know he left here to meet her," he says.

"How do you know what they texted about?" I ask, curiously.

"Our phones are connected to Red's network; he doesn't spy on our calls, but the texts are monitored and in times like this it's extremely helpful."

"Why is it helpful?"

"I need you to be calm when I tell you this," he begins. I nod, "Okay."

"We don't think Taylor is who she says she is."

"What do you mean?" I ask, as calmly as I can.

"We're not sure yet, but isn't it odd that she only asked

Colt to come last night? Why didn't she reach out to the rest of us?"

"I don't know why, but I'm sure we could ask her. Let's just go ask her."

"I don't think that's the wisest decision," he says, calmly.

"Why?" I ask, irritation creeping into my voice.

"We traced both of their phones. They were in the same spot last night, but only Taylor's phone left, and she hasn't mentioned Colt once this morning. So, we need you to play dumb with us. You don't know any of what I just told you, okay? I need you to do this, so we can figure out what happened. I wanted you to be aware of what was going on. You can trust us, and I don't want you to think we're hiding anything from you, okay?"

He looks at me, genuine concern on his face and I know Colt was right. These are people who would do anything for each other.

I nod, "Let's do this."

CHAPTER TWENTY-FOUR

Colt

My head is pounding, and I can barely see out of my left eye, but I'm alive. Tied up, but alive. I'll take it, that means I can still kill this bitch.

You know the evil people who talk about their plans too much? Well, when you do that, you should make sure the person you're talking to is dead or is going to be dead.

I'm definitely not dead and I have no plans to die.

She's been playing Cassie from the beginning. She's an FBI Agent, she didn't lie about that. What she did lie about is the fact that she's been obsessed with Jay since high school and she's resented every woman that got in her way. She is the person who's been recruiting women for his trafficking business. Women see a woman with a badge, and they let their guard down. She brings them to Jay, and he distributes them as he sees fit.

It's nauseating, but she was smiling the whole time she was blabbering away.

Everything was going great for her, until Cassie. Cassie wasn't someone who asked how high, when Jay said jump. Cassie was a challenge, an obsession.

No matter what Taylor did it was never enough because

Cassie was the only person he could think about. She said that's when she decided to put her plan into action. She began to leave little clues for other Agents to find about Jay's business. As they closed in on him, she helped him stay a few steps ahead of them. Then when a task force was created to keep tabs on Cassie, she volunteered. She made sure to insert herself into not only every aspect of the investigation, but Jay and Cassie's life. She figured if she could get Cassie out of the picture then she would be Jay's number one again.

She hired us and a few other hitmen to get rid of her. It was a perfect plan, until she noticed the connection between Cassie and me. She knew something was up with us, because we'd been in the bar a few times and avoided other women like the plague, for the most part. But, when Cassie came in and spent the night talking to me, she knew I was going to be a problem. She also realized we weren't normal people.

That's when her plan needed to change and that's why I'm here now. She told me this is where I'm going to die, but the bitch is wrong. I'm getting out.

I rock the chair and strain against the binds on my ankles and pull at the ones on my wrist.

"Ah, ah, ah. I wouldn't do that if I were you," a deep, male voice rumbles from behind me.

CHAPTER TWENTY-FIVE

Cassie

"Are you okay?" Taylor asks, as soon as we walk into the living room.

"Yeah, I was just having some problems getting dressed. You know, you've got to love the day after pain," I joke.

"Damn, I cannot wait to get my hands on him and make him pay for everything he's done," she says, angrily.

If I didn't know the truth, I'd believe her. Inside my stomach is churning, but I know what I need to do, so instead I reach out to hug her.

"Thank you, Tay. You're the best. I don't know what I would do without you."

I keep my eyes lowered to the ground. I know if I look directly at Ike or Chris I'll break. I step away and look around the room.

"So, what's the game plan for this morning? Is Colt out getting breakfast?" I ask, as nonchalantly as possible.

Ike goes to speak, but Taylor holds up her hand. "Now, sweetie, don't freak out, but we can't find Colt."

I never realized it before, but she baby talks me sometimes and it annoys the shit out of me. Of course, it may annoy me more now that I realize what and who she is, but I'd like to believe it's always bothered me, I just never vocalized it because I wanted to be nice.

"We were talking this morning and the last place Red was able to track his phone was here at the house. That's what Red is doing right now, trying to figure out what the hell happened that he can't track Colt's phone."

Interesting, they are playing it very close to the chest. They don't even want her to believe they know where his phone is.

"Whoever has him, we'll find him," she continues. "I mean, Red is a bad ass computer guy. I can't imagine someone would best him."

I inwardly groan, is she really praising herself right now? She is way more fucked up than I originally believed.

"Yes, he is, but in the meantime what can we do? Colt wouldn't just leave in the middle of the night for no reason," I say, worriedly. That's not fake either. I have no idea what she's done to or with him.

"Well, I was kind of talking something out with him last night before we left. Maybe he couldn't sleep and decided to investigate it on his own," she says, hesitantly.

"Well, what were you talking about? I mean if it's something that could help, I think we should check it out," I say, firmly.

"Are you sure?" Ike asks.

"I don't think we have any other options right now," I shrug, "And I can't be here, while he's out there somewhere."

He nods in agreement.

"Okay, then let's do this," Chris chimes. "Where are we going?"

"I'll drive," she smiles.

CHAPTER TWENTY-SIX

Colt

My body freezes as I try to get a glimpse of who's behind me.

"Is this the infamous, Jay, I've been hearing so much about?" I taunt.

My head jerks back, as he grabs the top of my hair and pulls. "I don't know, is this Colt? The man who thinks he can have what belongs to me?"

"She belongs to no one," I grimace. "She can be with whoever she wants to be with. It just so happens, that person is me."

"You see, that's where you're wrong. She doesn't want to be with you. She wants to be with me, she just doesn't realize it yet. That's why I'm here, to make her remember," he sneers, stepping around to face me.

"How crazy are you, man?" I ask. "I mean, you must be certifiably insane, right?"

"Would an insane person do this?" he asks, pushing my chair over.

"Fuck! Yes, they would asshole," I yell.

"I guess that makes me insane then," he grins.

"Well, next time you do this to someone, I'd recommend

you not do it. Mainly because, when you knocked me over, yes, it hurt like a bitch, but you also broke the wooden chair you put me in."

I push myself off the ground. "You and your little girl toy need to plan shit out better from here on out. Unfortunately, I don't think that will be an option for you very much longer. Also, who the fuck uses pure wooden chairs anymore?"

"I do and she isn't my girl toy, she's someone who will do anything I ask. She's loyal," he says, circling me. "But, if you want those to be your last dying words, by all means, let those be your last words."

I want to hold my ribs to help stop the pain, but it consumes my whole body. Instead, I push past the pain and focus on the man intent on killing me.

"You're hurt pretty badly," he grins. He pulls out a small knife and flips it in his hand. "This is going to be fun and easy."

He's arrogant, he's going to make a mistake. I watch his footwork and his hands, to try and see where he's going to move next. He jabs right and I'm able to dodge it, but he immediately swipes at me again and connects with my arm

I try to ignore the pain and blood flowing from my body and focus on him. I reach out throwing a quick jab and connect, but at the same time, he swipes me across the stomach.

I grimace and try to keep fighting, but I know the look I'm giving off. It's one of a wounded prey. If he's anything like me, he's going to pounce soon.

I can feel the end of things. I fall to my knees.

"You're weak," he snarls. "You don't deserve to have her."

He drags the knife across my upper arm, then plunges it into my shoulder.

"I will always be a better man than you," I grind out.

"That may be, but I'll be alive, and you'll be buried six feet under the dirt. So, does it really matter?" He asks, as he pulls the knife out and then stabs me in my lower back.

"You talk to much," I moan.

"You die too slowly. This is no longer amusing for me," he says. He pulls out a gun and I drop my head.

"Goodbye, you won't be missed, Colt."

"You're wrong, I will be, and you'll never have her," I stammer.

I close my eyes and wait for the sound of the gun to go off.

EPILOGUE

Cassie

It's been six months since I walked in on Jay shooting Colt. I don't think it's something you ever forget. The sound of the gun, the smell of the blood. The sight of a lifeless body of someone you love. It's imprinted on you forever.

We walked in as Jay was about to shoot Colt and I remember screaming so loudly as the gun went off and Colt's eyes meeting mine for a brief moment.

In that moment, I tried to convey everything I felt for him. Tried to tell him thank you for everything he gave me in the short amount of time we had together.

You aren't always blessed to have an instant connection with someone, but when you do, you think it will last forever. It was supposed to last forever for Colt and me, but Jay and Taylor took it away from us.

As I watched Colt fall to the ground that day, I remember trying to think of the best way to hurt them for taking Colt from me. But, I couldn't. It wasn't and isn't in my nature.

It should have been though, they deserved it. Taylor lied to me for years. She betrayed my trust, used my vulnerability against me and I fell for it. Hook, line and sinker. She said she was my friend, but all this time, all she wanted was Jay.

Jay, all he wanted was power. Power over whoever and whatever he could get. He didn't care about you once he had you. He just wanted to make sure he could get you. The fact that I turned him down so many times, drove him crazy. I was one of the very few people that ever told him no and didn't wind up dead.

They probably do deserve one another.

I didn't need to worry about revenge though. Chris and Ike went off. I stood there frozen, but they went crazy. Ike attacked Taylor and Chris went after Jay.

I wanted to help, but I couldn't. My heart was broken, and the pain just permeated through my body. Ike pinned Taylor down and had her cuffed. He told me to stay still and that there were more people coming, I didn't know what he meant, but I knew I could stay still.

I watched as he went over to help Chris trap Jay and as Jay laughed, rage flew through me.

I remember calling out to Jay, and the sound of my voice distracting him. As soon as he looked at me, Ike knocked him out. When Taylor saw him fall, she let out the most primal scream I'd ever heard.

I looked at her and said, "Now maybe you can begin to understand how I feel."

Those were the last words I said to her, before she was taken into custody.

Now, their trial is beginning. Not only is the trial for Jay and Taylor, it's also for the guy who attacked me. They managed to get my attacker, thanks to Red. He made sure they saw the video surveillance that had been illegally placed in my home. With all the evidence against them I was able to make a deal with the district attorney to give my testimony via a video deposition, so I didn't have to testify in court in front of them. Every time I think about having to see them again, I go into a full-blown panic attack.

I moved out of my condo and Red, Ike and Chris were nice enough to take me under their wing. I was lost after I lost Colt. I thought I had finally found happiness and it was ripped from me. I had no direction and I wasn't sure where I was going to go or what I was going to do.

The guys understood my dilemma. They'd all been in a similar position before. So, they brought me along for the ride.

Now, I help research their cases before they take them on. They rented a little office space for me to work out of, that doubles as a small living space and the guys check in with me for assignments.

I also took over Colt's position in trying to help Red find what he's lost. It helps give me a purpose. If I can do that, I'll feel as if I finished what Colt intended to do. I know that may seem stupid to some people, but for now that's my purpose. It will continue to be my purpose.

I'll always miss him, but despite everything I gained a family and I'll do anything to protect them.

ALSO BY IVY LOVE

Lost in Me, Found in You
Cutting Through the Darkness
Belle's Goodbye

<u>Quinn Winters Novels</u>
A Killer Past
Silenced

ABOUT THE AUTHOR

Ivy is a lover of reading, writing, high heels and animals.

When she isn't writing, she is either working in the legal field or playing with her four dogs. When she was in grade school, she was your classic nerd. She spent more time reading books "above her grade level" and getting lost in them, instead of paying attention to the people around her. She loved the journey each book would take her on, she still does. When she was thirteen, she picked up a pencil and wrote her first hundred-page story. It was the moment she realized she could not only lose herself in books, but in her own words. That was the moment she fell in love with writing.

She writes because she must. She has stories to tell and wants to share them with all of you.

www.booksbyivy.com

Made in the USA
Columbia, SC
13 October 2022